Space Poop

A funny rhyming story about poop in space.

Written and Illustrated By

Krista Tarasyuk

An astronaut had a funny look on his face.

There, out the window, was a turd floating through space.

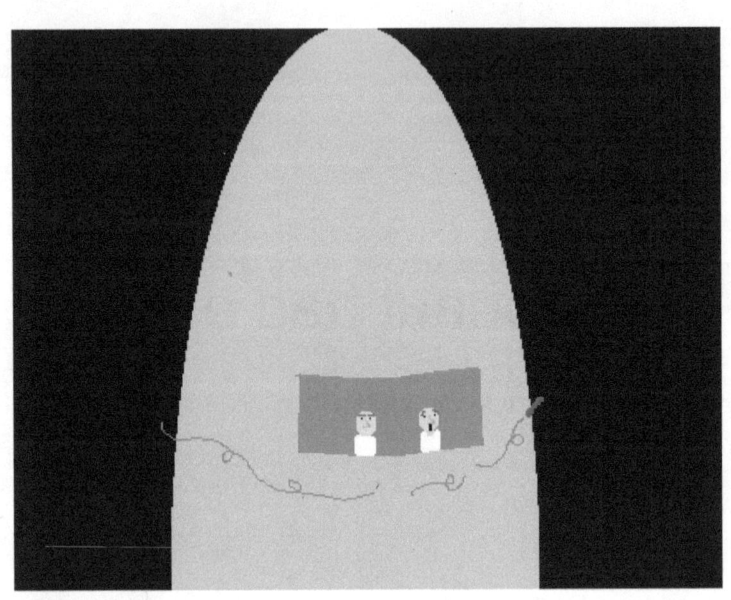

The poop looked fresh
because outer space is
so cold.

He could not determine
if it was new or old.

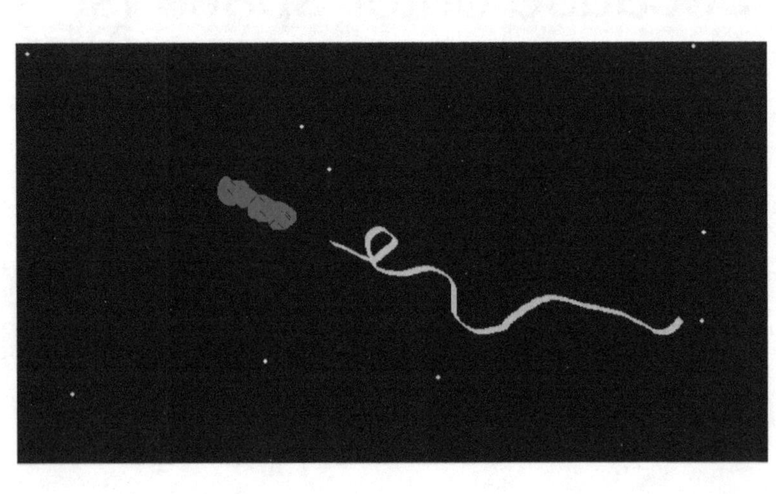

"How old do you think it is?" The astronaut asked.

The other astronaut looked.
Then, he laughed.

"A space poop!
I thought I had seen it all!"

He started to make
a radio call.

“NASA, I hope you are seeing this too!

You wouldn’t believe it! We have found space poo!”

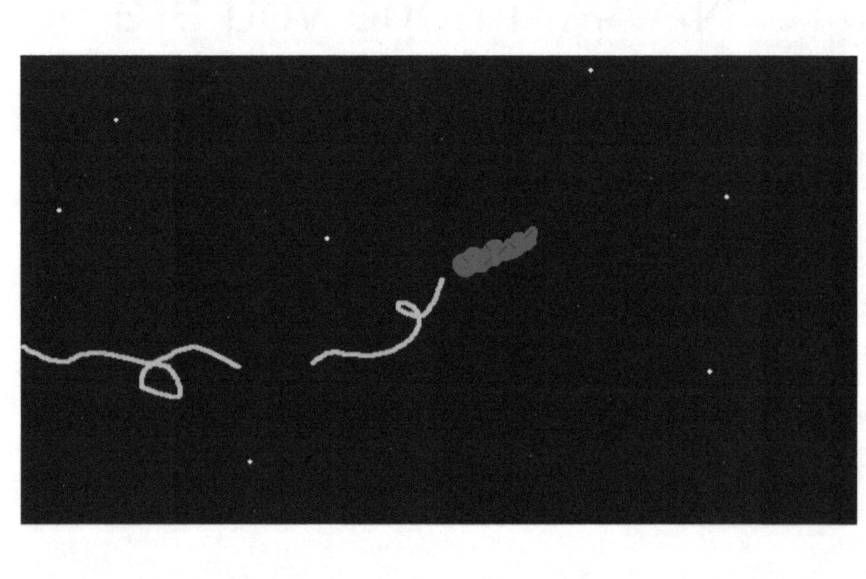

NASA responded,
“We already know!

The astronauts in the past had “to go”.

They would do their business, then seal it away.

Sometimes a poo would go astray.

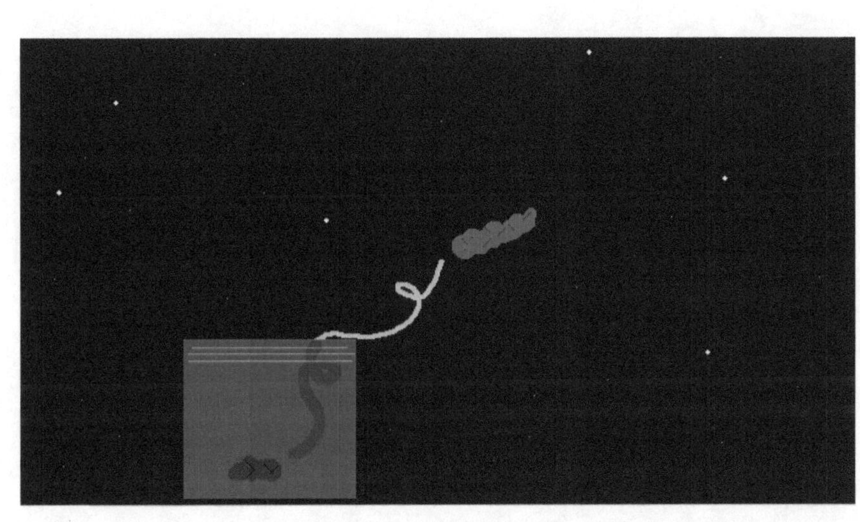

The astronauts giggled.
“I know it’s not mine!”

They stared at it as it floated- frozen in time.

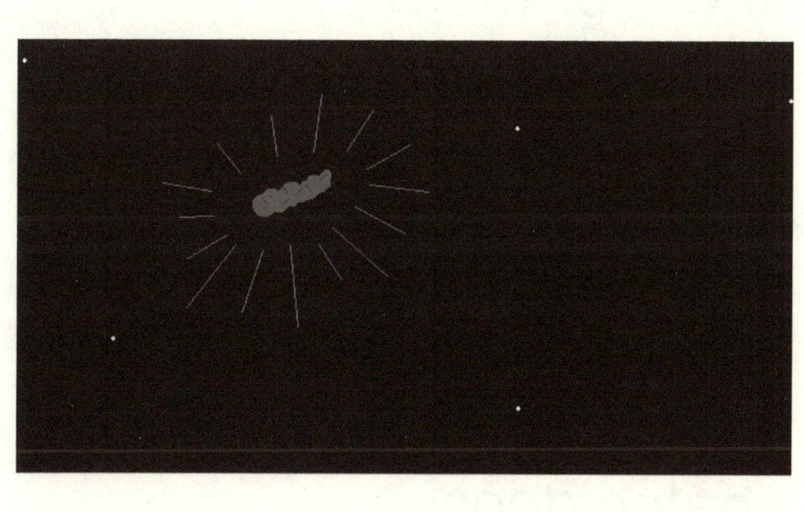

After looking at it for an hour or more,

They decided to open the hatch door.

They swam through space to catch the poo.

They knew it was the right thing to do.

After their mission was finally done,

They returned back to Earth-

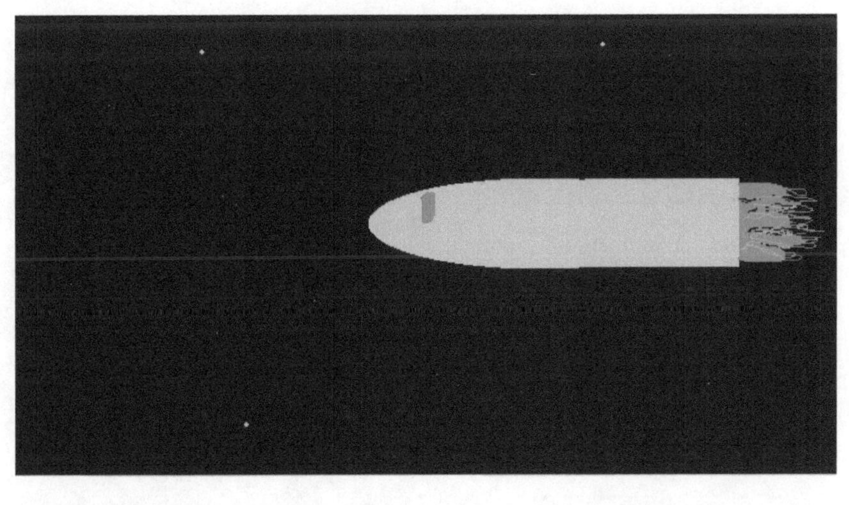

With the space dung!

This story was *inspired* by a real incident that happened during Apollo 10. Eugene Cernan, Tom Stafford and John Young discovered a turd (then, a second one) floating through their vessel. Although this story is different, it is still fun to think that if one can escape from a feacal disposal bag, it could *also* escape from an open hatch as they exit into space accidentally. They would never even know it! Astronauts today *could* make a poop discovery even though it is *highly* unlikely. This story is **not** a true story and was written for entertainment purposes only.

www.ingramcontent.com/pod-product-compliance
Lightning Source LLC
LaVergne TN
LVHW041307150826
845673LV00008B/2784

* 9 7 9 8 8 1 0 8 3 8 5 2 4 *